NOT ME!

Nicola Killen

D1390451

C153879116

EGMONT

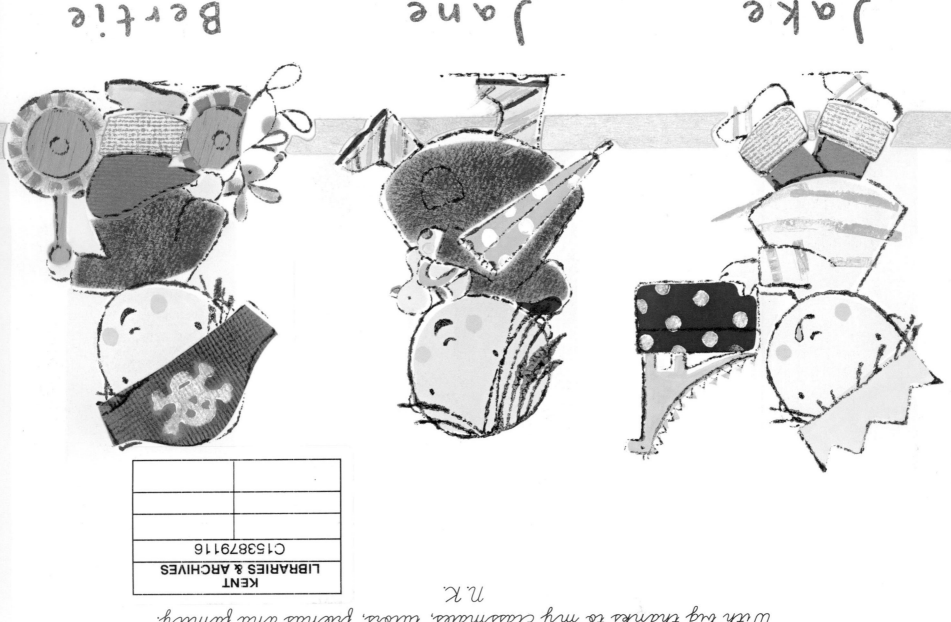

Bertie

Jane

Jake

KENT LIBRARIES & ARCHIVES	
C153879116	

With big thanks to my classmates, tutors, friends and family.

U.K

NOT ME!

Nicola Killen

Paul   Louise   Jess the Pup

eating

all the cake?

NOT ME!

said Jake.

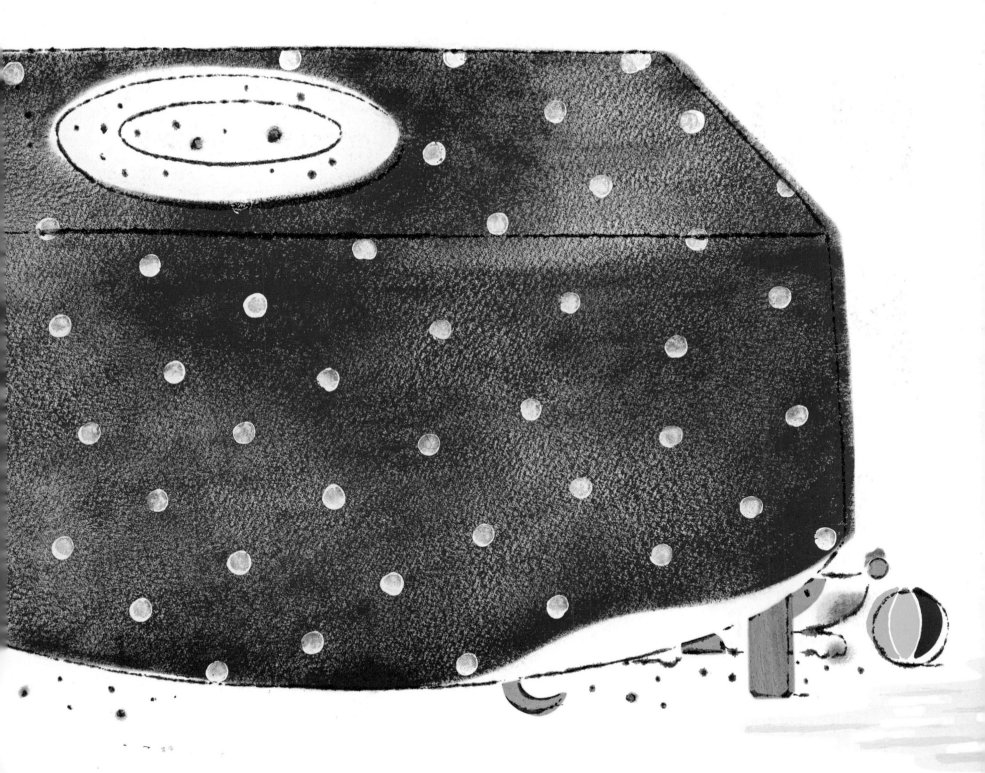

Who's been **playing** in

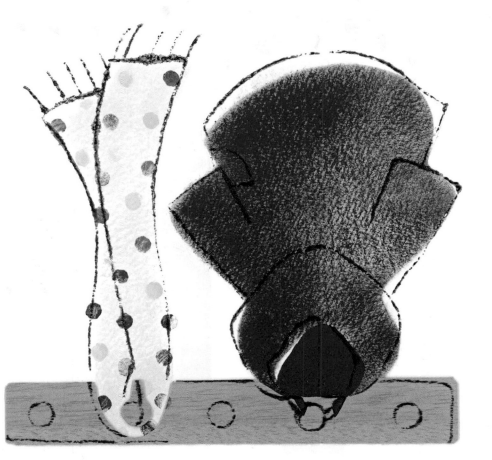

the rain?

NOT me!

Who's been
MAKING
the carpet dirty?

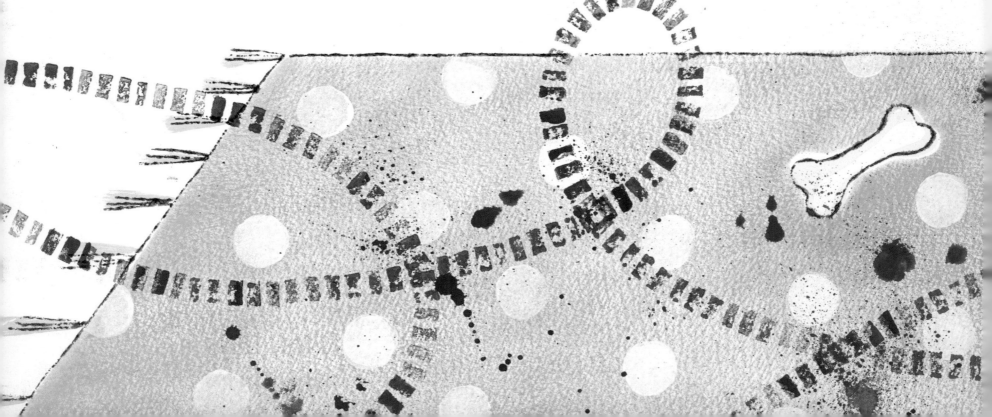

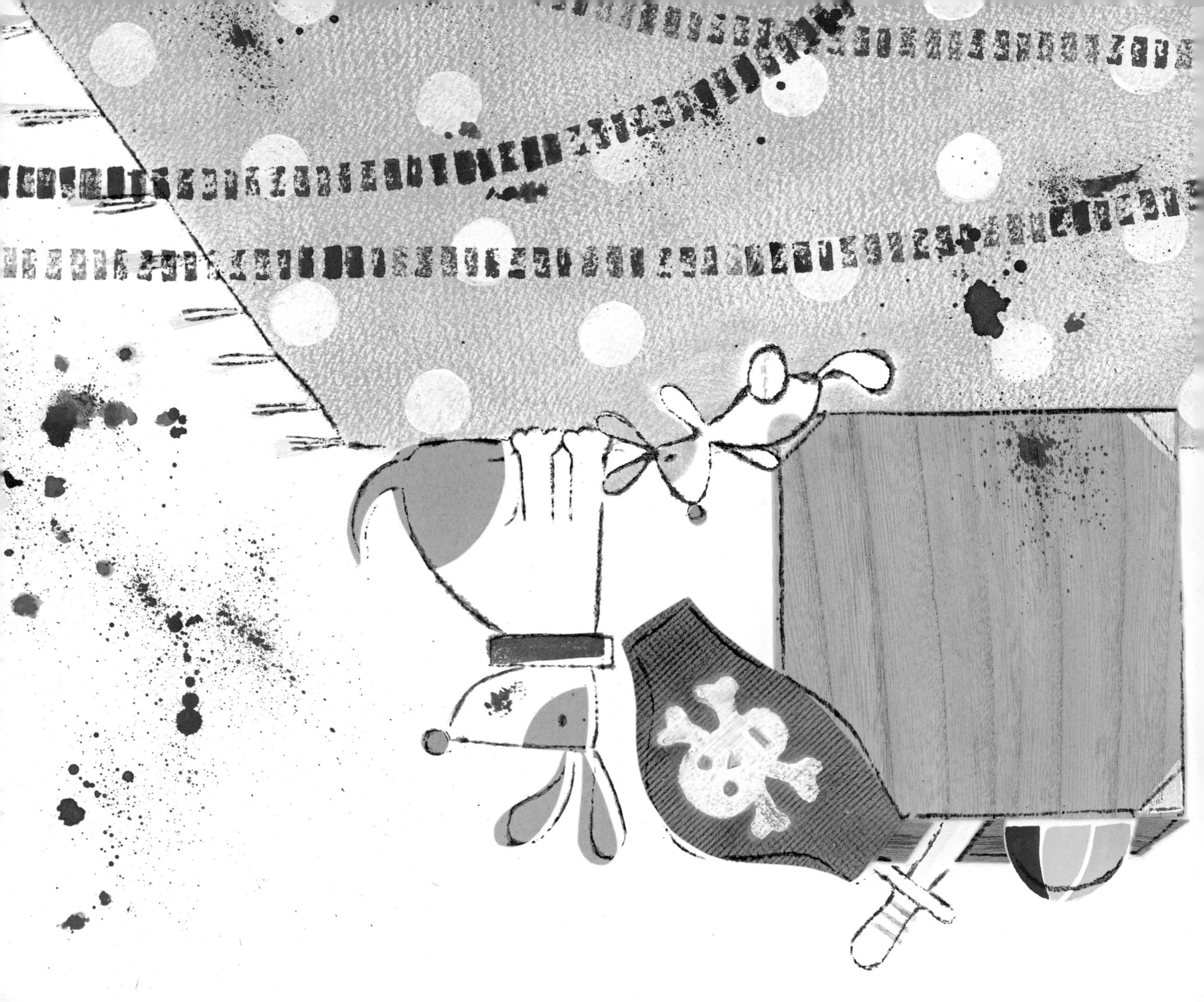

said Bertie.

hand prints on the wall?

NOT me!

said Paul.

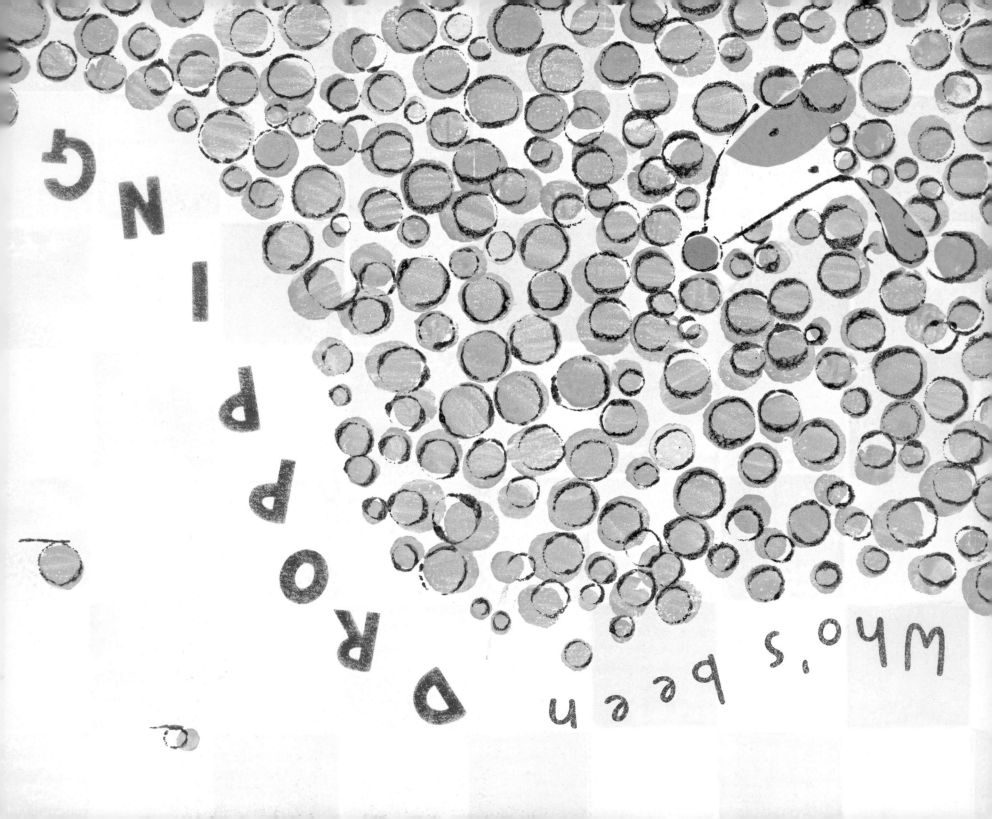

all these peas?

Not Me! said Louise.

So who's been making all this MESS?

CAN'T YOU GUESS?!

But who's

going to **CLEAN** and **TIDY UP?**

NOT ME!

thought Jess the Pup.

First published in Great Britain 2010
by Egmont UK Limited
239 Kensington High Street
London W8 6SA

Text and illustrations copyright © Nicola Killen 2010

The moral rights of the author/illustrator have been asserted

ISBN 978 1 4052 4829 7 (Hardback)
ISBN 978 1 4052 4830 3 (Paperback)

1 3 5 7 9 10 8 6 4 2

A CIP catalogue record for this title
is available from the British Library

Printed and bound in Singapore

All rights reserved. No part of this publication may be reproduced, stored in a retrieval system, or transmitted,
in any form or by any means, electronic, mechanical, photocopying, recording or otherwise,
without the prior permission of the publisher and copyright owner.